This book is dedicated to all animals on this earth,
whatever their colour or shade.

This paperback edition first published in 1995 by Andersen Press Ltd.
First published in Great Britain in 1993 by Andersen Press Ltd., 20 Vauxhall Bridge Road, London SW1V 2SA.
Published in Australia by Random House Australia Pty., Level 3, 100 Pacific Highway, North Sydney, NSW 2060.
Copyright © Max Velthuijs, 1993.
The rights of Max Velthuijs to be identified as the author and illustrator of this work
have been asserted by him in accordance with the Copyright, Designs and Patents Act, 1988.
All rights reserved. Colour separated in Switzerland by Photolitho AG, Offsetreproduktionen,
Gossau, Zürich. Printed and bound in Italy by Grafiche AZ, Verona.

10   9

British Library Cataloguing in Publication Data available.

ISBN 978 0 86264 625 7

This book has been printed on acid-free paper

Max Velthuijs

Frog and the Stranger

Andersen Press · London

One day, a stranger arrived and made a camp at the edge of the woods. It was Pig who discovered him first.

"Have you seen him?" asked Pig excitedly when he met Duck and Frog.

"No. What's he like?" asked Duck.

"If you ask me, he looks like a filthy dirty rat," said Pig. "What does he want here?"

"You have to be careful of rats," said Duck. "They're a thieving lot."

"How do you know?" asked Frog.

"Everyone knows," said Duck indignantly.

But Frog wasn't so sure. He wanted to see for himself. That night, when darkness fell he saw a red glow in the distance. Frog crept nearer.

At the edge of the wood he saw a couple of sticks with a rag draped over them, like a makeshift, untidy tent. The stranger

was cooking in a pot over a fire. There was a wonderful smell
and Frog thought it all looked very cosy.

"I've seen him," Frog told the others, next day.
"And?" asked Pig.
"He looks like a nice fellow," said Frog.
"Be careful," said Pig. "Remember he's a dirty rat."
"I bet he'll eat all our food without ever doing a day's work,"
said Duck. "Rats are cheeky and lazy."

But that wasn't true. Rat was always busy. He collected
wood and skilfully made a table and bench.
He wasn't really dirty either. He often bathed in the river
although he looked a little scruffy.

One day, Frog decided to visit Rat. Rat was sitting resting on his new bench in the sun.

"Hello," said Frog. "I'm Frog."

"I know," said Rat. "I can see that. I'm not stupid. I can read and write and I speak three languages – English, French and German."

Frog was very impressed. Even Hare couldn't do that.

Just then, Pig arrived.

"Where are you from?" he asked Rat angrily.

"From everywhere and nowhere," replied Rat calmly.

"Well, why don't you go back?" cried Pig. "You've no business here."

Rat remained calm.

"I have travelled all over the world," said Rat unmoved. "It's peaceful here and there's a wonderful view over to the river. I like it here."

"I bet you stole the wood," said Pig.

"I found it," said Rat in a dignified voice. "It belongs to everyone."

"Dirty rat," muttered Pig.

"Yes, yes," said Rat bitterly. "Everything is always my fault. Rat is always blamed for everything."

Frog, Pig and Duck went to visit Hare.

"That filthy rat must leave," said Pig.

"He's no right to be here. He steals our wood and is rude as well," cried Duck.

"Quiet, quiet," said Hare. "He may be different from us, but he's not doing anything wrong and the wood belongs to everyone."

From that day on, Frog went to visit Rat regularly. They sat side by side on the bench, enjoying the view and Rat told Frog stories of his adventures round the world, for he had travelled widely and had had many exciting experiences.

Pig disapproved of Frog.
"You shouldn't go round with that filthy rat," he said.
"Why not?" asked Frog.
"Because he's different from us," said Duck.
"Different," said Frog, "but we're all different."
"No," said Duck. "We belong together. Rat isn't from round here."

Then one day, Pig was careless while he was cooking.
Flames leapt from the frying pan. Soon the fire spread and the
flames were everywhere. The house was ablaze.

He ran outside terrified. "Fire! Fire!" he screamed. But Rat
was already there. He hurried between the river and the
house with buckets of water and fought the flames until the
fire was out.

The roof of Pig's house was totally destroyed. All the animals stood round in shock. Now Pig was homeless. But he needn't have worried. The next day, Rat came round with a hammer and nails. As quick as a flash, the house was repaired!

Another time, Hare went to the river to fetch some water.
Suddenly he slipped and fell into deep water.
Hare couldn't swim.
"Help! Help!" he shouted loudly.
It was Rat who heard the shouts at once and dived straight
into the water. Quickly he rescued Hare and brought him to
the safe, dry bank.

Everyone now agreed that Rat could stay. He was constantly happy and cheerful and was always there if someone needed

help. He often thought of fun things to do like having a picnic by the river or a trip into the forest.

And during the evenings, he told them all exciting stories about dragons in China and other exciting things he had encountered in the world. It was a very happy time and Rat always had new tales to tell.

But one fine day when Frog visited his friend Rat he couldn't
believe his eyes. The tent had been taken down and Rat was
standing there with his rucksack.
"Are you leaving?" asked Frog in amazement.
"It's time to move on," said Rat. "I might go to America. I've
never been there."
Frog was devastated.

With tears in their eyes, Frog, Duck, Hare and Pig said
goodbye to their friend Rat.
"Perhaps I'll come back one day," said Rat cheerfully. "Then
I'll build a bridge over the river."

Then he left – that filthy dirty, but nice, cheeky, helpful, clever
Rat. They stared after him until he disappeared behind the hill.
"We'll miss him," said Hare with a sigh.
Yes, Rat left an empty space behind. But the bench was still
there and the four friends often sat together on it and talked
over their memories of their good friend Rat.